© LEGO

© LEGO

© LEGO

© LEGO

© LEGO

© LEGO

© LEGO

© LEGO

© LEGO

© LEGO

© LEGO 7

© LEGO 7

© LEGO 7

© LEGO 7

4

4

© LEGO

© LEGO

© LEGO

© LEGO

© LEGO

© LEGO

© LEGO

© LEGO

© LEGO

© LEGO

© LEGO

© LEGO

4

4 **4**

4

© LEGO

© LEGO

© LEGO

© LEGO

© LEGO

Get ready for another amazing adventure with the LEGO® NEXO KNIGHTS™!

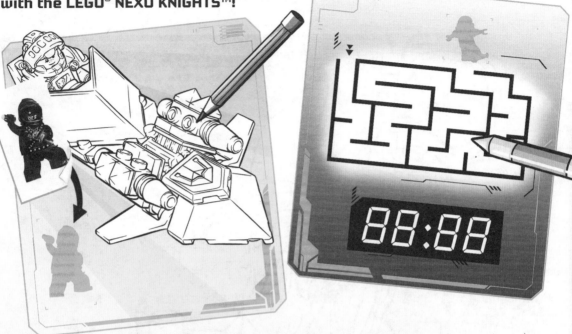

Find the right sticker to match the silhouette on each page.
Then colour in and complete the awesome activities.

You'll find all the answers on pages 62-64.

This is Merlok 2.0 – the best (and only) digital wizard in Knighton! Find the right squirebot sticker to complete the scene and then colour in the picture.

The NEXO KNIGHTS heroes' shields are essential in the fight against Lava Monsters! Add the shield stickers, then draw a line to connect them to their rightful owners. They can't download NEXO Powers without them!

The Knights' Academy Library rules include: no eating, no talking and, most importantly, NO MONSTERS ALLOWED!

Use your stickers to create a scene where the monsters are running away from the NEXO KNIGHTS team, and Marge, the persnickety librarian!

Greedy Jestro forgot that his Evil Mobile can only carry a maximum of ten tonnes of cargo. Add up the numbers on the chests below to discover which one he should leave behind. Then find the missing sticker to add to the page.

Ava and Robin are upgrading the Fortrex's operating system. Put your symbol stickers in the empty boxes so that each one is connected to another symbol of an identical shape.

The Book of Monsters is hungry. The mere thought of a *Ned Knightly* comic book is making his mouth water. Can you draw a line to the exact issue he is thinking about, and add a sticker of Jestro to the page?

12 12 12

15 15 15 15 15 15 15 15 15

16 16

16 16

12 12 12 12 12

9

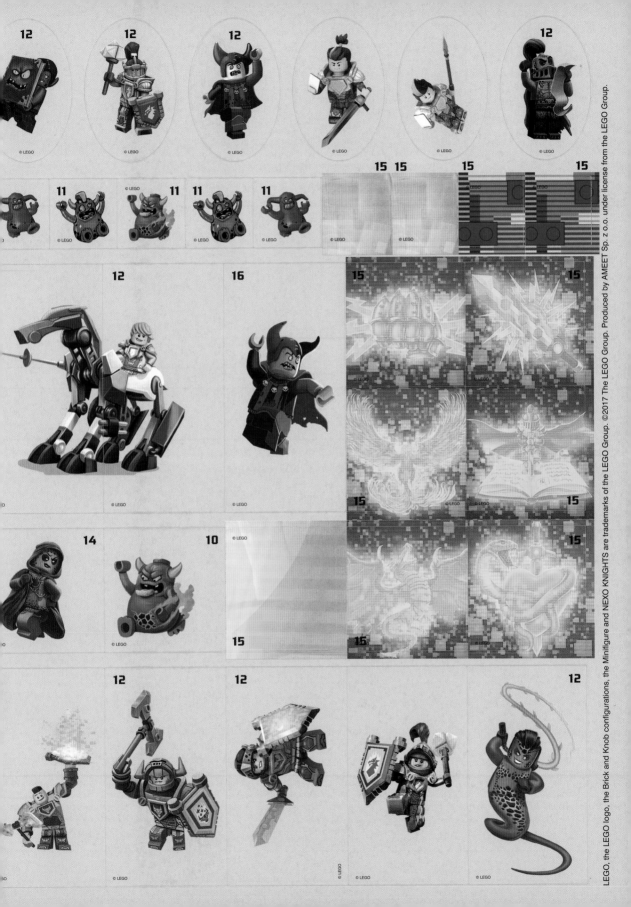

12 12 12 12

© LEGO © LEGO © LEGO © LEGO

11 11 11 11 11

© LEGO © LEGO © LEGO © LEGO © LEGO

15 15 15 15

© LEGO © LEGO

12 16 15 15

© LEGO © LEGO 15 15

14 10 15

© LEGO © LEGO

15 15 15

12 12 12 12

© LEGO © LEGO © LEGO © LEGO

Robin the inventor has created the Minitrex – a rolling fortress combined with a comfy suit of armour. Colour it in and then find a squirebot sticker to add to the page when you are done.

When General Magmar starts reading out his list of orders, it's time to grab a book, or a crossword, or – even better – take a nap. Look at the pieces below and find the one that doesn't match the picture.

When you have as many pages as the Book of Monsters, it's easy to be disorganized. Use your stickers to solve the puzzle so that there is only one of each type of monster in every row, column and 4x4 square.

When it's the king's birthday, Jestro celebrates it like it's his birthday too . . . by crashing the party! Use your stickers to play out a heroic battle between the Knights and the Lava Monsters.

Don't forget to add a sticker of the cunning Book of Monsters to the battle scene too!

To stand any chance of winning the 'Deliciously Dangerous Hottest Chilli Cook-Off Contest', Axl needs a special ingredient. Untangle the lines to discover which chilli should go in the pot, and then colour in the scene!

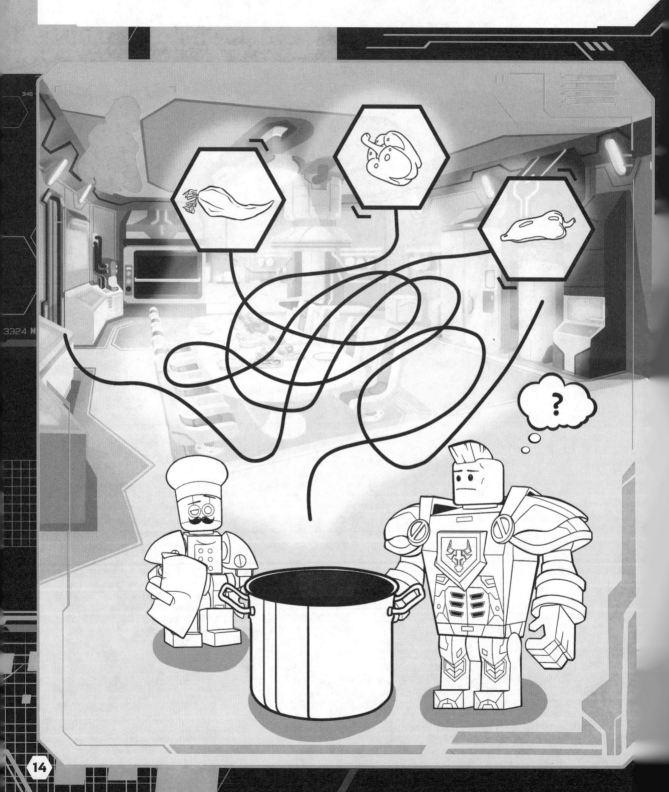

Depth Charge, Fist Smash, Rock Ripper . . . there are so many NEXO Powers. Each one is fantastic in its own right. Now it's your turn to design a new shield with a new power. Write an awesome name for it in the box!

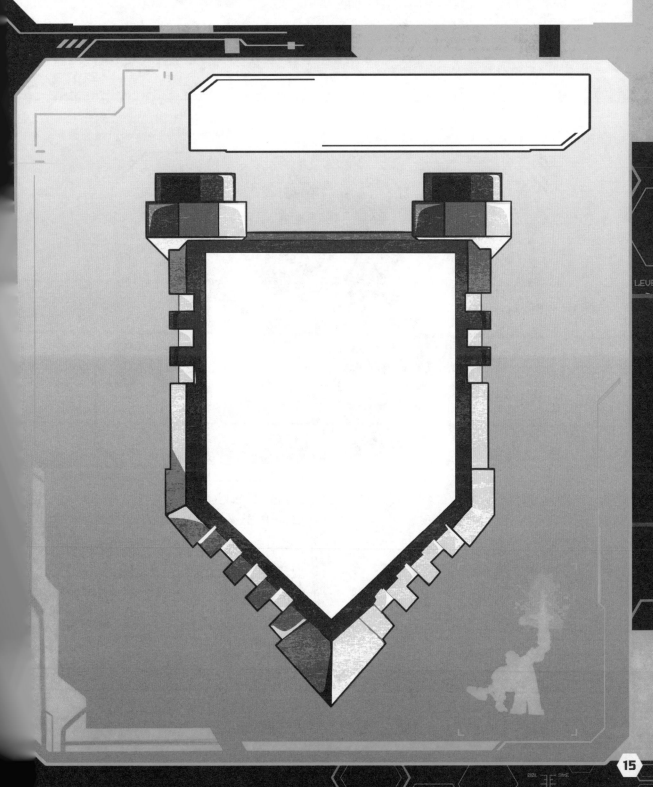

Use your NEXO Power to find the right stickers to complete the jigsaw puzzle. Then find a Jestro sticker to put on the page.

© LEGO   © LEGO   © LEGO   © LEGO   © LEGO   © LEGO

© LEGO   © LEGO   © LEGO   © LEGO   © LEGO   © LEGO   © LEGO   © LEGO

© LEGO   © LEGO   © LEGO   © LEGO   © LEGO   © LEGO

© LEGO   © LEGO   © LEGO   © LEGO

© LEGO   © LEGO   © LEGO   © LEGO   © LEGO

© LEGO   © LEGO   © LEGO   © LEGO   © LEGO

20

23 23 20 20 20 20 20

18 18 18 20 22

20

20 19 24

18 18 18

20 20 20 20 20

Axl should be training with Clay but he's stopped for a snack attack!
Circle everything in the picture that he needs for his training session
and then find a sticker of Clay to complete the page.

The Fortrex is an all-in-one rolling fortress, command centre and war machine! Build it with your stickers on the grid below.

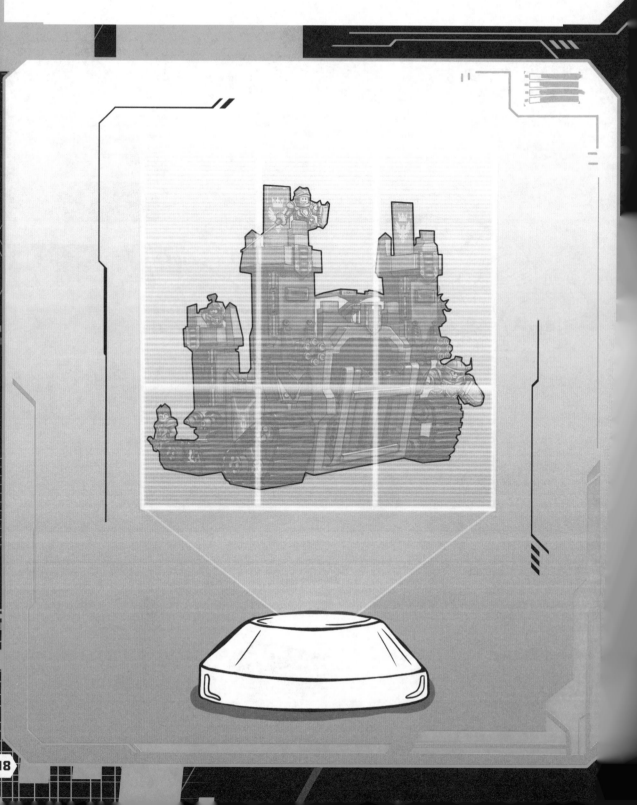

The NEXO KNIGHTS team has the Fortrex, but Jestro has the Evil Mobile, which is powered by pure monster muscle! Colour it in and complete the page with a sticker of a Lava Monster.

The Book of Monsters has caught a cold. Now every every time he sneezes, slimy green monsters appear in the forest. Yuck!

Find stickers of the NEXO KNIGHTS heroes to add to the scene so they can battle the snotty monsters!

LEVEL

21

Oh no! The Fortrex's operating system has been infected! Help Ava find the virus inside the source code shown on the screen. Clue: the virus' code is shown inside the white block below. Then find a sticker of Robin and his spanner to fix the problem.

Axl is ready for a fight – watch out, yucky monsters!
Find the right hexagon to match the missing section on Axl's Tower Carrier,
then colour the vehicle in. Reward yourself with a yummy cake sticker
when you are done.

True NEXO KNIGHTS heroes can take care of themselves in any situation, even without their weapons! Draw lines to connect the objects in their hands or on their armour to the ones on the floor. Then colour them in and find a Globlin sticker for the page.

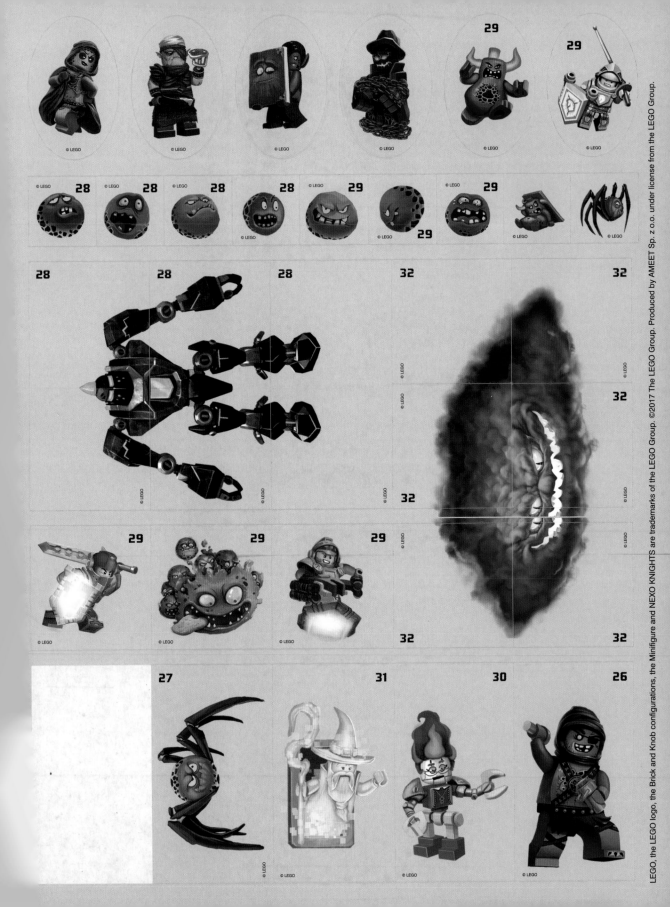

Watch out! The Book of Monsters is trying to get hold of the Book of Betrayal. Untangle the lines to find out which of the Knights is going to reach the tricksy book first. Then stick the Book of Monsters on the page.

No one can keep up with Aaron when he's at the controls of his Aero Striker!
Colour in his mean machine and find a sticker of Beast Master
to add to the page.

The Book of Monsters decided to do a trial run before summoning Monstrox. It turned out to be a good idea because one of the monsters appeared twice! Find it, then stick a Spider-Globlin on the page.

LEVEL

It's the final showdown in the Lava Lands! Who will win? You decide.

Find a sticker of Marge the librarian to add to the page. Then draw lines
from the books on the trolley to the spaces on the shelves
so that every row looks identical.

Behold: Techalibur – the sword filled with Merlok's power. It's the only weapon that can stop the Book of Monsters from summoning evil Monstrox! Colour in the sword with your mightiest pencils, then find the sticker to match the silhouette.

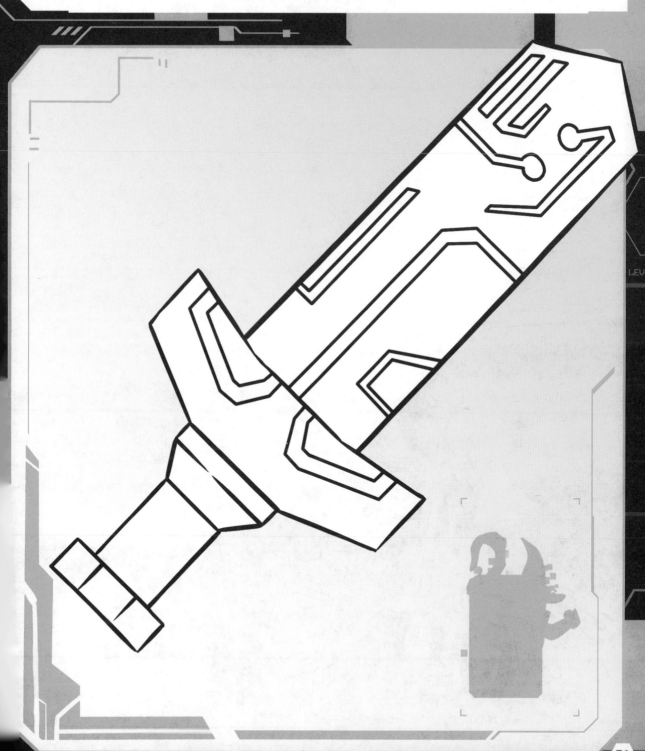

LEVEL

The NEXO KNIGHTS heroes are thrilled that the Book of Monsters has finally been defeated! But they don't realize that another enemy is already lurking in the background! Do you know who it is? Add in the sticker parts to find out.

40

39

33

38

37 37 37 37 37

37 37

36

34

35

The Book of Monsters may be gone, but the Cloud of Monstrox is here! One zap of his lightning was enough to get Jestro on his side. Draw the mighty bolt that struck the poor jester, then find the sticker to match the silhouette.

NEXO Powers aren't enough to stop the Stone Monsters.
The Knights need something special to defeat them – a COMBO POWER!
This time it's the Shield of Lightning Ultra Armour. To discover who
downloaded it, find the Knight with the same shield icons.

This is Clay's new vehicle, the Falcon Fighter Blaster. Colour the picture to make his new machine look even more amazing. Then add a sticker of Clay to complete the page!

It's not only Clay who has a new machine – the other Knights
have awesome vehicles too.

Put stickers of their vehicles on the page so they can show them off,
then find a squirebot to stick in the scene.

LEVEL

Lance Richmond is taking part in a reality show about the lives of the NEXO KNIGHTS heroes. But he doesn't want the others to know! Can you draw circles around the ten hidden cameras Lance has put inside the Fortrex before Macy finds them and gets angry? Then find the sticker to match the silhouette.

**The artist Arnoldi is trying to complete a memory challenge but needs your help. First, find a sticker of the missing statue, then look very closely at the picture and all the elements in it.
Now turn the page.**

Circle six things in the picture below that appeared on the previous page. No cheating! Then find the sticker to match the sword silhouette.

© LEGO

© LEGO

© LEGO

© LEGO

© LEGO

© LEGO

© LEGO

© LEGO

© LEGO

© LEGO

© LEGO

© LEGO

© LEGO

© LEGO

© LEGO

© LEGO

© LEGO

© LEGO

© LEGO

© LEGO

© LEGO

© LEGO

© LEGO

© LEGO

© LEGO

© LEGO

© LEGO

© LEGO

© LEGO

© LEGO

© LEGO

© LEGO

45

42

45

46

41

47

43

48

45

45

45

45

45

45

45

45

45

Perhaps Robin's new invention will liven Clay up a bit? He's been acting a little stiff recently. Colour in Clay's Battle Suit and then find a sticker of a squirebot.

Introducing Jestro's new Rolling HQ. Isn't it great?
Of course it isn't, it's evil! But the most important thing
for Jestro is that it performs well in battle.

Can you spot twelve differences between these pictures?
Then colour them in and find stickers to match the silhouettes
on both pages.

Rockwood is no ordinary forest – you'll find
a terrifying army of Stone Monsters lurking there!

Use your stickers to create a battle scene between the NEXO KNIGHTS heroes and the Stone Monsters. Robot Hoodlum and his Merry Mechs can join in too!

Robot Hoodlum's Merry Mechs are fixing broken squirebots.
Look at the picture and match the bots to their missing parts.
Then colour in Robot Hoodlum and find a sticker to match the silhouette.

All the Knights have their own Battle Suits. Colour in Macy's suit so she looks awesome when she goes into battle against the monsters. Then find a sticker of Axl to complete the page.

The Stone Brothers are annoyed as everyone keeps getting their names muddled up. Untangle the lines to discover which letters are missing from their names and vehicle. Then find a sticker to match the silhouette.

R U ◇ B L E

R O O ◇

R E X ◇

G

H

I

M

L

E

54 54 54 54 54 54 54 54 54

53 53

LEGO, the LEGO logo, the Brick and Knob configurations, the Minifigure and NEXO KNIGHTS are trademarks of the LEGO Group. ©2017 The LEGO Group. Produced by AMEET Sp. z o.o. under license from the LEGO Group.

49

51 51 51 51 51

54 54 54 54

52 52 52 53 50

53

55 52 52 51 52

56 53 53 53 53

LEGO, the LEGO logo, the Brick and Knob configurations, the Minifigure and NEXO KNIGHTS are trademarks of the LEGO Group. ©2017 The LEGO Group. Produced by AMEET Sp. z o.o. under license from the LEGO Group.

Squirazzi seize every opportunity to take pictures of Knightonia's celebrities. Untangle the lines to see who they are trying to catch on camera this time. Then colour in the bots and find a sticker of a squirebot to complete the page.

Oh no, the queen has been kidnapped by the Electric Witch and trapped inside the Lock & Roller! Help Clay chase down the kidnapper! Colour him in, find the way through the maze and add on the missing sticker.

FINISH

START

Use a black pencil on all the number '1' shapes and a purple pencil on the number '2' shapes to reveal the hidden monster. Leave all the number '3' shapes white, then find a sticker to match the silhouette.

Yikes! The Cloud of Monstrox has brought to life every statue in the king's garden! Now the NEXO KNIGHTS heroes are in real trouble . . . unless you help them!

Quick! Use your stickers to create an epic battle scene between the NEXO KNIGHTS heroes and the Stone Monsters!

ANSWERS

p. 3

p. 6

p. 7

p. 8

p. 10

p. 11

p. 14

p. 16

p. 17

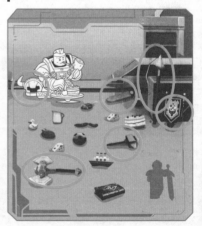

p. 22

p. 23

p. 24

p. 25

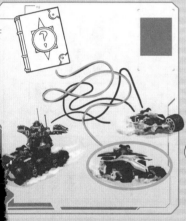

p. 27

p. 30

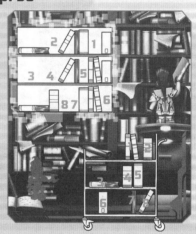

p. 34

p. 38

p. 40

pp. 42-43

p. 46

p. 48

p. 49

p. 51

p. 54

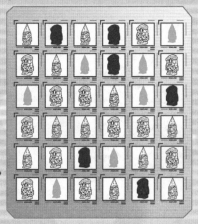

p. 57

p. 58

p. 59